ODD ONE OUT

To Elizabeth, my best friend
To Flavie and Leah too.
D. C.

To Edith.
I.

AUZOU Books
24 -32 rue des Amandiers 75020 Paris, France.
ISBN 978-2-7338-5066-4
LCCN or Library of Congress info

First published as L'ABOMINABLE by Les éditions de la courte échelle inc.
Copyright © 2013 Les éditions de la courte échelle inc.
Les éditions de la courte échelle inc. 160, rue Saint-Viateur Est, bureau 404
Montréal (Québec) H2T 1A8

Original Text by Danielle Chaperon
Artwork by Iris
English Translation by MaryChris Bradley

For children 4 years of age and up.

Printed in China

Danielle Chaperon

ODD ONE OUT

Illustrations by
Iris

AUZOU

My life turned upside-down one terrible, dreadful day last spring. Up until then, I'd been entirely happy.

I had parents who loved me.

I had a younger brother who was still too little to bother me.

And we lived in a house that was big enough for the four of us, *plus*, my entire insect collection.

But best of all, I had Annabelle... ah, Annabelle Hart! My wonderful, brilliant, *very* best friend!

She was as beautiful
as an angel.

She cooked
like a master chef.

She always made me laugh.

And when she ran, she was faster than
a shooting star.

Yes, Annabelle had everything but best of all
she had me, Clara. I was her *very* best friend.

We were inseparable.
We spent our days together.

We stuffed our faces
with chocolate.

We would imitate our favorite singers.

We even got bored together.

My parents said that we were soul sisters.

I don't know what that means, but it sounded nice…

And then, on that horrible, awful day, *the new girl* walked into our classroom! Of course, our teacher told us to be nice to *the new girl*.

The new girl sat down next to Annabelle, and Annabelle *smiled* at her!
In the beginning, I wasn't worried. I was sure that nothing could come between Annabelle and me.

And then things got worse!

Annabelle and *the new girl* walked
to recess hand in hand!!!

ARGH... I could barely breathe...
My knees went weak...
How could this be happening?

My heart sank.

Oh Annabelle, I can't believe it. It's horrible! The absolute worst has come to pass, *the new girl* is now Annabelle's *new friend*!

But there can't be *THREE* soul sisters! It is clearly, absolutely, and mathematically impossible!

THREE can't walk together on the sidewalk!!! There's not enough room. I was the odd one out who trailed behind with tears in my eyes.

THREE can't fit on a bike, it's too dangerous!!!
I was the odd one out who rode alone.

I felt as if I'd begun to shrink... and shrivel...
until I was *very, very, very* small.

Before long, I'd be invisible

So I decided to come up with the perfect, diabolical plan to get rid of *the new girl.*

Diabolical Plan No. 1
Buy a witch's potion that would transform the new girl into a disgusting, stinky rat!

But where would I find a witch?
Are witches even real?

Diabolical Plan No. 2
Invite the new girl *over to my house, then*
when she isn't looking,
dump my entire insect
collection on her!

But my insects might like *the new girl*
and leave me.

Diabolical Plan No. 3
Take a chance and just ask
Annabelle to choose between
the new girl *and me.*

But what if she picks *the new girl*?
ARGH!

Instead I did nothing at all.

I just sat on the bench in the hallway and cried.

Then there was an accident.
An incredible, extraordinary accident!

The three of us were at the park when Annabelle's kite
got caught in a *very, very*, tall tree.

Before I knew it, I was climbing the tree.
I went higher… and higher… trying to rescue her kite
when suddenly the tree limb broke, and I tumbled to the ground!

OUCH!

Later that afternoon—after my parents brought me home from the doctor's office—Annabelle came to visit me.

She gave me a gigantic, enormous box of chocolate covered cherries. *My favorite*. Yum!

Then *the new girl* arrived. She handed me a small box. Inside was an adorable little bug who wiggled his antennas at me.

How lucky am I?
I got **two** excellent gifts from my **two** best friends:
That's when I realized that **two** best friends are
twice as nice as just one...

And my best friends, Annabelle Hart
AND Juliette Branch, are the *BEST* of all!